Dedications

For my husband Padraic,
and my daughter and son
Ciara and Adam.

With all my love xx

Printed by Lightning Source Ltd.

Paperback ISBN: 9781838537241
Hardcover ISBN: 9781838537258

A Connemara Fairy Tale

Words by Nicola Heanue
Illustrations by Zoe Saunders

At the bottom of the trees, hidden by moss and brambles, on a little farm in Connemara, you will find the Fairy homes of a family of Gnomes.

The head of the family is Norbert the Gnome, and his beautiful red-haired wife Noreen.

The gnomes take care of the animals on the farm.

They have lots of animals to care for, including the farm's very special herd of Connemara Ponies. The gnomes make sure there are no tangles in the ponies' manes or stones in their hooves.

In exchange for their help, the ponies allow the gnomes to use their old horse-shoes to make special doors for their Fairy Houses.

Life was good for the gnomes and all the animals on the farm, until one night, a very strange thing happened.

Norbert and Noreen were woken by the sound of galloping hooves in the fields.

The noise woke all the farm animals – the cows were mooing, the hens were clucking, the sheep were baaahing – and it seemed that no gnome would be able to nod off to sleep.

As daylight dawned, a gang of grumbling, grouchy, grumpy gnomes went to the fields to find the ponies still sleeping, with daisy chains around their necks and tangles in their manes!

The fields were destroyed, hoof prints everywhere and tracks of mud around the walls. Norbert was furious and an angry gnome is never a good thing! He woke the ponies and demanded that they explained their behaviour, but the ponies could remember nothing.

Their muscles ached and they felt very tired but none of them could remember their midnight gallop around the fields. Nobody could explain where the daisy chains had come from or why their lovely silken manes were knotted and tangled.

So who could be responsible for this midnight mischief?

'Oh no!', gasped Norman Gnome (Norbert's brother), 'these look like pesky pixie pranks to me'.

(Pixies are extremely small fairies who are generally well behaved but are sometimes known for causing mischief and mayhem).

'We need a plan to prevent these pesky pixies from playing pranks on our ponies', declared Norbert.

It was decided that the gnomes would keep lookout the following night and see if they could catch the pack of pesky pixies.

Sure enough, as the sun set and all the animals on the farm were settled down for a nights' sleep, the gnomes spotted the pack of pixies picking their way through the fields to where the ponies lay.

As the pixies tried to mount the ponies, the gnomes slid down their silken manes and landed right in front of the pesky pixies.

It was Paddy Pixie and his pack of pesky pixies, playing pixie pranks on the ponies.

'You have destroyed our fields, terrorised the
ponies and tangled their silken manes',
grumbled a grouchy, grumpy Norbert Gnome.
'But why?'

'We galloped around the fields at night
Simply for our own delight',
replied Paddy Pixie.
'The daisy chains we used as reins,
but the knots are just for mischief'.

'We are seashell shining pixies
who live on the seashore,
but the waves came crashing in
and our seashell homes are no more',
he added sadly.

Norbert and Norman and all the gnomes
pitied the pixies for the loss of their fairy
homes but this did not excuse them for
their pranks on the ponies.

All fairies need jobs to keep them busy and
out of trouble, so the gnomes just
needed to find something for
the pixies to do.

They all headed back to the gnomes' homes on the farm. When they reached the little gnome town the pixies' faces lit up with delight as they saw the gnomes' wonderful horse-shoe fairy doors.

The gnomes explained where the shoes for the fairy doors came from and how they were extra strong and sturdy to keep them safe and warm in their homes.

'Every Fairy house should have a magical horse-shoe door to protect their homes from the wind and the rain', declared Paddy Pixie.

And so it was decided that the pixies would help create the doors while the gnomes continued to care for the ponies in exchange for their shoes.

And from then on, instead of pesky, prank playing pixies, they became polishing, painting and fairy door producing pixies who travelled to all the fairy festivals around Ireland to sell the fairy doors.

The Author

Nicola lives in Connemara with her husband Padraic, daughter Ciara and son Adam, their dog and their herd of Connemara Ponies.

There are also a number of gnomes and pixies living in her garden who Nicola sometimes helps with their fairy door production.

Connemara
Therapeutic Riding

Connemara Therapeutic Riding was founded in 2015 to provide a service for local children and adults with special needs. Together with the community and support from various agencies, Connemara Therapeutic Riding was born.

CTR provides an all inclusive, Family Experience with Sibling Sessions and some much needed Respite for parents/carers while their children are safe in the hands of the Fully Trained and Qualified Coaches. The therapy ponies at CTR are all Registered Connemara Ponies, bred, reared and trained in Connemara . They have proven to be the perfect therapy pony, calm and placid, seeming to innately understand what is required of them. CTR is funded entirely by grant aid and the continuous efforts of a fundraising team.

10% of the proceeds from A Connemara Fairy Tale will go directly to Connemara Therapeutic Riding.

All proceeds from Connemara Fairy Doors go to CTR, for which they are very grateful to the Gnomes and Pixies.

Lightning Source UK Ltd.
Milton Keynes UK
UKHW051258250920
370502UK00003B/15